THE PLAY
OF THE WEEK

THE PLAY
OF THE WEEK

AND OTHER SPORTS STORIES
Compiled by the Editors
of
Highlights for Children

BOYDS MILLS PRESS

Compilation and jacket illustration copyright © 1993
by Boyds Mills Press
Contents copyright by Highlights for Children, Inc.

Published by Boyds Mills Press, Inc.
A Highlights Company
815 Church Street
Honesdale, Pennsylvania 18431

Publisher Cataloging-in-Publication Data
Main entry under title.
    The play of the week : and other sports stories / compiled by the editors of
Highlights for Children.
[96]p. : cm.
Stories originally published in *Highlights for Children*.
Summary: A collection of sports stories.
ISBN 1-56397-193-3
1. Sports stories—Juvenile fiction. [1. Sports stories.]
I. Highlights for Children. II. Title.
    [F]   1993
Library of Congress Catalog Card Number: 92-73626

First edition, 1993
Book designed by Tim Gillner
The text of this book is set in 12-point Garamond.
Distributed by St. Martin's Press

10 9 8 7 6 5 4 3

CONTENTS

CONTENTS

The Play of the Week

By Linda Berry

"Hey, Jennifer!"

"Good pass!"

"Yippee!"

The voices from the soccer field usually made Allison hurry to join her teammates, not wanting to miss a minute.

Today, instead, she inched her ball with her foot carefully around a bush and through the open gate onto the field.

As she arrived, the coach was dividing the boys and girls into small groups for drills. Good. Allison didn't want time to talk to anybody today. It was her fault that her team, the Roadrunners, had lost Saturday's game with the Jets.

Usually Allison enjoyed every minute of practice, but today she found herself watching her teammates to see if they were angry with her. Did Luis kick that one out of her reach on purpose? Did Andy mean to bump into her like that? Why wouldn't Jennifer pass to her?

Allison had even thought of pretending to have a sore throat or stomachache or something to keep from coming to practice today. The funny thing was, she almost *did* have a stomachache from thinking about it. She hoped the stomachache would go away after she faced up to the team.

The coach's whistle broke into her thoughts.

"OK, boys and girls. Oranges!" This call signaled to them that it was time to talk over practice and the last game.

Slowly Allison dribbled her ball over to the group. She tried some extrafancy juggling, almost hoping she'd miss and have to chase the ball far away from them.

"Good practice, kids," the coach said after they had settled down on the grass and the oranges had been devoured.

Then, as usual, he checked his clipboard and made comments to each player. Allison braced herself.

"Erin, your dribbling is really improving. You're going to surprise those Fireballs Saturday! Allison, keep working on control. You're one of our strongest halfbacks."

Whoosh! Allison let out the breath she'd been holding. At least she was past *that*. Maybe the coach wouldn't say anything after all.

"Now, about last week's game."

Allison drew in another breath. It wasn't over yet.

"You looked good and played a good game. The Jets are a tough team. Let's see where we could have done better. Jennifer?"

Jennifer laughed and said, "Man on man!" That was safe. They always needed to work on that.

The coach agreed with her. "Right! What else, Freddie?"

Freddie thought a bit and suggested, "Position. I know when I got out of position, the Jets got through and really put pressure on the goalie."

Again the coach agreed. "I'm glad you understand that. Good, Freddie."

"Now for the play of the week," the coach was saying. "Who has a suggestion?"

This was something the boys and girls always enjoyed. Several hands waved.

"Erin?"

"I think it was when Luis went in to cover the goal and blocked that shot close to the goal box."

There was loud applause at this suggestion. The coach nodded. "Any other suggestions?"

Andy said, "I think the best play was Freddie's steal from that big guy on the Jets and then passing the ball to Jennifer to score."

The youngsters murmured approval. The coach said, "That was a beautiful play, and it shows how important teamwork is. Good! Any others?"

There was silence as the boys and girls thought. When nobody had any other suggestions, the coach spoke again.

"My recommendation for play of the week isn't either of those." The teammates looked at one another in surprise. Those two plays had been the most dramatic of the game.

"Do you remember in the second half when several players were bunched up near our goal and the ball went out of bounds?"

They all remembered. That was just before the Jets made the goal that broke the tie and won the game. Allison began to squirm.

"Do you remember that the referee called it out on the Jets?"

Yes, they remembered. Some of the athletes glanced at Allison. That stomachache was still there.

"Do you remember that Allison raised her hand and corrected the ref, saying that *she* had knocked it out?"

How could they forget? That throw-in by the Jets

led to a long pass and a strong kick and the winning goal. Even having Jessica in position in the goal couldn't stop it! Now several boys and girls were looking at Allison more openly. She couldn't look up.

The coach continued. "You know team, I call what Allison did the play of the year, not just the play of the week."

The boys and girls raised a questioning murmur.

The coach explained. "Winning a game unfairly or by mistake doesn't tell us anything about how good a team we are. We play to do the best we can and see how we stack up against other teams. Right?"

The group was quiet now, most of them looking down at the grass. Several players nodded agreement. The coach wasn't quite through.

"Keeping the record straight and honest is the most important thing this team could ever learn about playing the game. I'm proud of Allison."

There was a pause, and then—"Let's hear it for Allison!"

The whole team joined in with "Hip, hip, hooray!"

Funny about that stomachache. Some back-pounding and a few friendly words were just the medicine it needed.

THE CHAMPION

By Dale Wagner

Honestly, a kid sister is the pits.

Lisa's cute, but she's a real nuisance. Dad expects me to take her everywhere.

So here I am, on my way to the most important hockey game of my life, with my seven-year-old sister beside me trying to keep up.

"Can I carry your skates, Bri?"

I hated being called Bri.

"No," I said.

"Oh, please, Bri," she pleaded, pulling one of the skates.

Snap! I tripped as the lace broke, and Lisa, still holding the skate, fell into a snowbank.

"Now look what you did!" I was angry. "How can I skate with a broken lace?"

"Let me fix it, Bri." She got up out of the snow. "I can tie a knot." She reached for the lace.

"Look, just leave me alone!" I pushed her away. "And when we get to the rink, don't call me Bri."

Lisa handed me the skate. I felt mean. But what could I do? She was being a pest. I tied a knot in the lace, and we walked the rest of the way without a word.

When we got to the rink, I found her a place where she could see everything. "Now sit here and don't bother me. OK?" I said.

Lisa nodded. She was smiling now, but I still felt mean.

I walked over to the rest of the players: six boys and six girls—the best hockey team around.

"How's your passing, Brian?"

"Hi, Carl. Janet and I practiced. Did you?"

"Naw. No time," he said.

No time? No time for hockey? Unbelievable!

I put on my skates. The knotted lace was OK.

"Hey! Red Riders!"

Coach Watson was calling us. We gathered in front of him.

"This is *the* game, team. We are going to be the Treeton County champs! Right?"

"RI-I-I-IGHT!" we yelled.

"We are going to win! Right?"

"RI-I-I-IGHT!" we yelled again.

"We are going to pass that puck! Right?"

"RI-I-I-IGHT!" We waved our hockey sticks over our heads and rushed out onto the ice, ready to win or else.

"Hi, Bri!" yelled Lisa, jumping up and down in excitement.

I didn't answer her. I didn't even look at her. I didn't need a fan club. No one else had a kid sister there.

I saw Carl look at her and then at me with a funny smile. He was laughing at me, I could tell. I didn't say anything. I just skated into position.

It was a good game. I played almost all of it, and I got two goals. We really played like a team. We all remembered where to skate and when to pass the puck. We did everything right.

Well, almost everything.

With two seconds to go in the last period, the score was 4 to 3. We were going to lose! Then Janet made a perfect pass so that the puck practically landed on my stick. I pushed forward. I would make the tying goal! But—I fell. Flat on the ice!

I jumped up, looking for the puck, but it was too late. The buzzer sounded. The game was over. We were not the champs.

Who tripped me? I wondered. Why didn't the

referee call the foul? And before I even finished the thought, I fell down again.

"OK," I muttered. "Someone is going to get it!"

But no one was around. No one except Carl, who skated over to me.

"Brian," he said. "What did you do? How could you miss that shot?"

By this time most of the team was gathered around me. I was too embarrassed to look at them, so I looked down. Then I saw the problem—the broken skate lace. The knot was untied, and the lace was dragging on the ice. The skate lace had tripped me.

Lisa broke that lace. It was her fault.

"Bri! Bri! Are you all right?" Lisa was pushing through the bigger kids around me.

"Go away, kid!" said Carl. He pushed her.

Lisa slipped and fell on the ice. In a second she was up and pushing harder through the crowd.

"I said go away!" said Carl, and this time he really pushed her.

"Hey, wait a minute," I said. "She's just a kid."

I got up and stumbled over to Lisa.

"OK?" I asked.

She nodded, blinking through her tears.

"Oh, Bri," she said. "I thought they hurt you. You fell so bad. And then you fell again. Don't be hurt, Bri."

Even though the other kids were watching, I

put my arm around her. I mean, what could I do? She was crying for me, not for herself, not because a bully had pushed her down, but for me. And she was just a little kid. So I put my arm around her.

"Hey," I said. "I'm OK."

She dug out a tissue and blew her nose.

"Let's go," I said.

"Hey, Brian!"

I turned. Oh no, I thought. Janet was skating over.

"Look, Janet," I said, "I'm sorry about your pass."

"No problem," she said, stopping in a spray of ice. "Great game, eh?" she said.

She was right. Up until my Great Fall, it had been great.

"Want to practice?" I asked.

"Sure," she said. "Who's your fan?"

"Oh," I said. And I stood a little straighter. "This is my sister, Lisa."

And I fell down.

That darn skate lace.

But this time we all laughed.

PLAY BALL!

By Stephanie Moody

Play ball!

Charyl's heart thrilled to the sound of those two simple words. Her eyes twinkled, and a grin lit up her face. Charyl loved to play ball, any kind of ball.

For her, summer was soccer and the smacking sound her foot made when she kicked the soccer ball with all her might. Fall was volleyball and the squeak of tennis shoes catching on the gym floor. Winter was basketball and the swoosh of baskets.

And spring? Spring was baseball.

Charyl frowned at the thought. Spring should be the crack of her bat against the baseball, sending it soaring. But spring was more like the swoosh of basketball, because Charyl always struck out.

"Easy out, easy out," the other team chanted when Charyl came to bat. Charyl knew they were right. She *was* an easy out.

"St-RIIIIKE three," the umpire hollered. "You're out!"

Charyl hung her head. She had done it again.

"Booo!" hissed the fans.

"Ooooooh," groaned her team.

"Why?" asked the coach.

Charyl didn't know why. There was just something about that little white ball growing bigger and bigger as it sped toward her, freezing her muscles, making her shake and swing wildly. If only she could close her eyes when she swung. Then it might be all right. But Charyl knew she shouldn't do that. A good player had to keep her eyes on the ball—always.

Grabbing her glove, Charyl raced to left field. At least I can catch and throw, Charyl told herself. A grounder didn't scare her. Catching a grounder was like trapping a little white mouse that scurried toward her, bumping and skipping over the field.

The roar of the crowd pulled Charyl's attention

back to the game. The second batter was already racing toward first base. For a brief moment the sun was behind a cloud, and Charyl knew the ball was coming her way. Knocking her cap from her head, Charyl searched the afternoon sky. Where? Where was it? Then she saw it looming over her head.

Charyl took two steps backward. She was ready. A fly ball didn't scare her. Catching a fly ball was like catching the moon as it hovered over her. Charyl waited until just the right moment, holding her glove steady. *Plop!* She had it. A well-placed throw sent it beaming toward second base. The second baseman made the tag. A double play!

Charyl jumped for joy. At least she wouldn't be warming the bench, not with a play like that. If only . . . if only she could bat.

Charyl's turn at bat came around faster than she wanted it to. She took a deep breath. She hated to bat. She hated the swinging, the missing, and the disappointment of striking out again. But most of all, she hated letting her team down.

"Just get a piece of it this time," her coach said. "Take a slice off that little ball. It's a piece of cake."

Charyl cocked her head, thinking. She knew "It's a piece of cake" meant something was supposed to be easy, but batting wasn't easy. At least it wasn't easy for her.

As the pitcher wound up, Charyl firmly gripped

the bat. "It's a piece of cake. It's a piece of cake. It's a piece of cake," she chanted over the jeers of the infield. And suddenly it *was*, because racing toward her was not the familiar hard ball but a big, white, fluffy cake. Charyl knew she could hit it. Anybody could hit a cake. It was too big to miss.

Crack! The bat slammed into the ball, sending it scampering toward third base like a frantic white mouse. Charyl was stunned. A cake goes *splat,* not *crack*. She had *hit* the ball. She had heard the sound she'd been waiting to hear all season.

"Run! Run!" urged her coach. Charyl dropped the bat and ran, pounding her feet down the base line. When she reached first, all her teammates were on their feet, cheering. Charyl couldn't believe her ears. They were cheering for her.

"Nice hit," yelled the first base coach.

"Piece of cake!" whooped Charyl, grinning from ear to ear.

The Race

By Sidney Pozmantier

Ellen was the first girl on the ready bench after she heard the announcement: "This is the first call for the eleven-and-twelve-year-old girls' 200-meter freestyle." Soon she was joined by other girls her age. She sat on the bench fidgeting with her entry card.

I hope I win, she thought. Then I will have enough points in the meet to win "Best Girl Swimmer" in my age group.

"Good luck, Ellen," said Nancy.

"Thanks," Ellen answered. "The same to you." She looked around for Amy Nelson, the only girl in the group who would be real competition for her. But Amy was not on the ready bench. Ellen remembered seeing her in the locker room thirty minutes before, so she was sure that Amy was in the crowd somewhere.

"Do you know where Amy Nelson is?" Ellen asked Nancy. "If she doesn't get here soon, she will miss the event."

"The last time I saw her she was over there," Nancy said as she pointed to a spot on the side of the bleachers. This was a favorite resting place for the swimmers as they waited their turn to swim.

Ellen's eyes slowly searched the group of girls for a glimpse of Amy. Finally, she saw her on the outskirts of the crowd. She was talking to a friend.

"This is the second call for the eleven-and-twelve-year-old girls' 200-meter freestyle."

Ellen watched Amy. She hadn't heard the announcement. Her conversation continued.

There's still time for me to get Amy, Ellen thought. If I run, I can be back before the last call for the event. She knew that without Amy's competition, she would surely win the event. After all, she reasoned, Amy isn't my responsibility. If she can't pay attention to what she is supposed to be doing, she doesn't deserve to win—or even be in the race.

Swimming had become a very important part of Ellen's life. She remembered her first swim meet when she was six years old. Then she wasn't even sure that she could make it to the other side of the pool—but she did. Coach had patted her on the back and said, "That was a good swim. You didn't give up. There'll be time for ribbons and winning later."

And that "later" came after many swim practices. Ellen never missed a session and never "goofed off."

At first she won fifth-place ribbons, and then slowly she worked herself up until she was winning first or second in each event she entered.

Lately she had been practicing extra hard so she could better her times and be eligible for the state meet next month. Coach had even given her permission to attend extra practice sessions with the older swimmers.

Ellen had a queasy feeling in her stomach. Her mouth was dry. But she knew this was more than ordinary jitters. I can't let Amy miss this event, she thought, and soon her feet were carrying her toward the other girl. She was out of breath when she reached Amy.

"Come on, Amy," Ellen said. "It's time for the freestyle. Hurry up before it's too late for both of us!"

The two girls raced to the ready bench. Amy

was the last girl to receive her entry card. "Thanks," Amy said to Ellen. "Guess I've learned something. I'll never again let my mouth get the best of me!"

All at once it was time for the last heat in the eleven-twelve freestyle—the fastest swimmers in the event. Ellen and Amy stood on their starting blocks next to each other.

"Swimmers, take your mark, set," BANG!

The girls hit the water.

Ellen's dive was good enough to put her ahead of all the other girls—except Amy. The two girls stroked—side by side.

In and out of the water went Ellen's arms, like a machine, and her legs kicked strongly. Slowly she edged ahead of Amy.

As Ellen approached the other side of the pool, her lead widened. Then Amy must have realized that she was falling behind and she began to work harder. Ellen's flip turn was sloppy, but Amy's was perfect. Soon the two girls swam side by side again.

One thought ran through Ellen's mind: I'm going to win. I'm going to win. By the middle of the third lap, Ellen forged ahead—little by little. Then she turned on the steam, executed a beautiful flip turn, and swam the last 50 meters, leaving Amy and the others far behind.

At last Ellen's hand touched the side of the pool. "I did it! I did it!" she shouted happily.

"You're a real friend," Amy said later to Ellen. "You

didn't have to come for me. Now everyone knows for sure you're the best swimmer."

"Thanks," Ellen said. She was glad that she had reached Amy in time for her to be in the race. Winning this event and the "Best Girl Swimmer" award was exciting, but winning fairly was the most important thing of all.

Making the Team

By Herman S. Adelson

Alan Merrill, baseball glove hooked through his belt, rode his bike up to the drugstore. In one motion he got off, leaned the bicycle against the rail, and hurried into the store.

"Hi, Mr. Brown," he called. "I need two packs of gum."

"Where are you going, Alan?" the pharmacist asked.

"They're having tryouts for the junior-high baseball team this afternoon."

"Listen, will you do me a favor on the way? I have

a prescription for Mr. Carver on Hilltop Road. He called and said he was out of his medicine. I want to get the pills up to him right away."

Alan hesitated. He wanted to be on time for the tryouts. Yet as a Boy Scout he felt obliged to help. He took the package and listened while Mr. Brown told him how to get to the Carver house.

"Give the doorbell a good long ring. He doesn't hear too well," Mr. Brown called as Alan left.

Alan rode off down Main Street, pumping hard on the pedals. I hope I'm not late for the tryouts, he thought. The notice on the bulletin board said 3:30. It must be three o'clock now. I can just make it if I hurry.

Around the corner, along Maple Street for three blocks, and there was Hilltop Road on the right. Alan made the turn at a 45 degree angle, trying to get a fast start up the hill. The street got steeper, and he had to shift into low gear. He was going well when ZAP! It happened so quickly that he had no time to brace himself. Over he went!

Alan lay there for a moment, stunned. Then he untangled his legs, pushed the bicycle away, and got onto his feet. Still a little shaken, he brushed the dirt off his clothes. There was a jagged tear in the knee of his jeans and another in his shirt sleeve. The skin on his knee and arm was scraped.

Well, he wasn't hurt too badly. What about the bike? He stood it upright and turned the pedal. It spun freely. The gears were stripped. He had fixed that problem before, but not without tools. Now what? He had to get the medicine to Mr. Carver. He couldn't leave the bicycle. There had been too many stolen bikes in town lately. He would just have to push the bicycle up the hill.

As he walked he thought, That fixes my chance to get on the team. I'll never get there on time now.

At last Alan reached 78 Hilltop Road. He leaned his bicycle on the grassy bank, trotted up the steps, and rang the doorbell. No one answered. He rang again. Still no answer. Leaning close to the door, he rang again. He could hear the chime of the doorbell and also the sound of music.

"That must be the radio," Alan said to himself. "He must be home." He turned the doorknob and the door opened. "Mr. Carver, Mr. Carver!" he called.

The sound of the radio came from a room just off the entry hall. Alan could see the radio on a table but the room seemed empty. He was turning away when something caught his eye. There was a hand hanging limply over the arm of the big chair.

In just three quick steps Alan ran to the chair and saw Mr. Carver slumped down in the corner. The boy gasped. Was Mr. Carver dead? No, there was just a flicker of an eyelid. Kneeling by the chair, Alan took the limp hand.

"Mr. Carver, wake up! Wake up! I brought your

medicine."

Mr. Carver's eyes slowly opened partway, and Alan felt a slight pressure from the hand. The man tried to form some words but nothing came out. Alan ripped open the paper bag and took out the bottle of tablets. He read the label. They were nitroglycerin tablets and the directions said: "Dissolve under tongue for chest pain."

"Do you want one of these?" Alan asked.

There was just the barest nod of the head, and Mr. Carver opened his mouth.

Alan unscrewed the cap, took out a tiny white tablet, and placed it in the man's mouth. "Shall I get you some water?" he asked.

Mr. Carver shook his head negatively but now his eyes were open wider, and he made a slight motion with his hand.

"Another tablet?" Alan asked.

This time there was a nod. Alan placed the tablet in the man's mouth, just behind the lower teeth. Mr. Carver closed his eyes, but Alan could see his chest move a little with his breathing.

Now what do I do? Alan wondered.

In his mind's eye he could see the back of the police cruiser: IN CASE OF EMERGENCY DIAL 911. He jumped to his feet, found the telephone, and dialed. Two rings later he heard a voice say, "Emergency."

Alan tried to speak slowly and clearly. "I am at

78 Hilltop Road. There is a very sick man here. I think it is his heart. Can you send an ambulance?"

"Seventy-eight Hilltop Road—an ambulance will leave immediately," answered the dispatcher.

Alan turned back to Mr. Carver. His eyes were open now and his breathing was deeper.

"I called for help," said Alan. "They're on the way."

When the ambulance arrived with siren and squealing brakes, Alan ran to open the door and then watched as the attendants put an oxygen mask on Mr. Carver. Except for asking the patient's name, no one paid any attention to Alan, so he went out the door and down the steps to his bicycle. Testing the hand brakes to make sure they worked, he mounted the bike and coasted down Hilltop Road, squeezing the brakes to control his speed.

At the ball field Alan's spirits dropped even lower when he saw that Coach Davidson already had the boys separated into groups.

I'm probably too late, Alan thought, but as long as I'm here, I might as well see what he says. He stood waiting to catch the coach's attention.

At last Coach Davidson turned and saw Alan standing there, with bruises, scrapes, and torn clothes.

"Hey, what happened to you?"

"I had an accident on my bicycle on the way

here."

"Why didn't you go home and get cleaned up?"

"The notice said 3:30 and I didn't want to be too late."

Coach Davidson nodded his head. "I see. You must be very eager to make the team."

"Yes, sir. I am."

"Good. It's important for us to have guys who hang in there when the going is tough. You go home and get those cuts and scrapes taken care of. Tomorrow we'll see what you can do with a glove and bat and ball."

The White Sox's Greatest Fan

By Casey Garber

They made my mom the manager.

None of the fathers would do it. "Too busy." So my mom said she would.

Then all the men offered to tell her all about baseball.

"No, thank you," she said.

When she told me, I couldn't believe it. I started jumping up and down. "No," I said. "No, no, no!"

"Yes," she said, "I'm afraid so."

I could just imagine what all the guys on the team would say about this.

And they did, too, because the phone began

ringing as soon as they heard. I groaned back and forth on the phone with four of the guys before bedtime.

On Saturday only half the guys showed up for first practice. This made the rest of us pretty mad. After all, it wasn't our fault we had a mother for a manager.

But all the team finally ambled in, and we had a decent practice. I mean, my mother was the White Sox's greatest fan. She grew up in Chicago, and she took it as a personal injury when they didn't win the pennant—which they usually didn't.

She knew more about baseball than most fans, and she could hit, catch with sure hands, and throw with a straight arm.

But the point was that no one else had a woman manager.

And the guys didn't know what to call her. Mostly they called her "Um." Like, "Um, should I stow the bats now?"

She said, "Call me *Coach*."

So we did. And she knew some things I didn't even know she knew. She'd read Ted Williams's book and she knew a lot about hitting. She gave us hints about stealing and how important it was to bunt well—especially when the other team didn't expect it.

Some of the guys thought this was a waste of time. They wanted to stand up there in the box and swing away. I know I did. I loved to get a good crack at the ball and watch it sail over the fence.

But my mom spent so much time on fundamentals—baserunning and sliding and squeeze bunts and turning the double play and beating out infield hits and making everyone pitch—that we felt we were going to lose the long ball. We sent a delegation to the coach.

Andy took the lead. "We feel, um, Coach, that we're not getting enough practice in the things we need."

"Oh?" she said, brushing a long piece of hair from her face. "Like what?"

"Like long-ball hitting—swinging away."

"We do have batting practice every day. Surely you've noticed."

"Yes, but—" He looked around at us for help, but none of us knew how to say it either. "I don't know."

"Well, if you come up with anything specific, I'd be glad to listen."

So we spent our time on the very basic fundamentals. And *all* of us pitched. I went home with my arm aching. I'd always played second and phooey on pitching, but, man, I was getting experience at it now.

Finally—our first game. We played the Homer Kings. Every year these guys were good. This year they took this name—Homer Kings—to show

how great they were. I have to admit I was scared. Not just that they'd beat us but that it would be a humiliation.

We were home team, so we took the field. That Matt Finkle, the fifth-grade smart-aleck, had a lot to say about the little sissies who had a woman manager. "What do you call her? Coach or coach*ess*?"

"Ha-ha," I called back. "Just you wait."

"What for?" he yelled. "Tea and cookies?"

Andy clenched his fist. Jake, our pitcher, spat on the ground, just like in the big leagues. We weren't sure about having a woman manager either, but we didn't want these guys commenting on it.

Anyway the game was going along OK till the sixth—we played seven innings in that league —except for the remarks from the Homer Kings. Andy was ready to fight. Once when Matt said something about white-lace fielder's gloves, I had to hold him back.

But we played to a scoreless tie, until Matt (naturally) hit Jake, our pitcher. He slammed that ball right back at Jake, who hardly had time to duck. The ball caught him in the chest and he went down with a big *Ooooff*. Knocked the wind out of him.

Oh no! I had to pitch.

I warmed up, and the old ball felt good. I struck out one and got another on a bouncer to third. But then the next batter hit one. I thought it was a good pitch; but it was a little high and he jumped on it. Hit it over the fence, in fact.

So now it was 1-0, and we had only two chances to go ahead.

We got a run in our half of the sixth with a single, a sacrifice fly, a bunt, and a stolen base —Andy stole home.

So it was 1-1, and there was a lot of hollering from the stands full of fathers who had all kinds of advice for us and our manager.

Once Andy turned around and yelled. But our coach said, "None of that."

Then they got another home run off me in the seventh. That made me so mad that I struck out the next three batters in a row. But it was 2-1, their favor.

Then it was our turn. David walked. Matt hit me with the pitch and I went to first. David took second. Jerry bunted safely, and we had the bases loaded. So no one could steal, except David. He could steal home. But since we had done that last inning, they'd be looking for it again.

We had to have something else fundamental besides stealing and bunting and walking and being hit. We'd done all that. We needed something new.

We got it. Hank hit a single, a nice, tight ball that skipped out to right field. David and I scored. We jumped up and down on the plate, and every-one ran and jumped on us. Especially Hank.

Then our coach told us to remember our manners, and we went over and shook hands with the Homer Kings and told them, "Nice game," and then we all went to my house for something to eat.

My mom sat down, and we waited on her. After all, she was the best baseball coach ever.

And we decided on a name for our team, too. The FUN-damentals.

The Magic Skates

By Aden Braun

Carl and Sandy Jensen trudged through the fresh snow on a morning hike to the pond. This was a new adventure for them. They were experiencing their first New England winter. They had lived in North Carolina before their father had been transferred to the new marine laboratory on Cape Cod.

Sandy and Carl each carried a pair of shiny new skates. Neither had ever ice-skated but they were anxious to try, since they were good roller skaters and skateboarders.

They arrived at the skating pond, sat down on a

fallen log at the clearing, and started to lace on their skates. A heavy blanket of snow covered everything, but the ice pond was completely clear.

"Who cleared it?" Sandy wondered out loud.

"Beats me," said Carl. He was bent over tightening his laces when he jumped up in surprise.

"New skates, eh?" said an old man as he peered over the top of his spectacles. He wore a battered hat, baggy trousers, and a long black overcoat. Behind his glasses were a pair of kind old eyes. "My name is Bunter, and this clearing is part of my backyard."

"How do you do, Mr. Bunter," Carl said. "I hope we aren't trespassing. My name is Carl Jensen, and this is my sister, Sandy."

"Well, happy to meet you." Mr. Bunter smiled. "You are not trespassing. All the children in the neighborhood use this area to change into their skates. See over there? That's where we have our bonfires at night."

"That sounds very nice," Sandy chimed in. "It's such a beautiful pond."

The pond nestled near the sea. A high bluff to the left and a jam of summer cottages to the right funneled the strong northerly winds along the salt marsh to the pond.

Mr. Bunter explained how the pond was kept clear. "The wind-whipped snow acts like a huge buffer that polishes the ice and leaves it clear of snow and silver smooth," he said. He chuckled when he added that many of the youngsters liked to think that he cleared it. He tried but couldn't discourage them from thinking so. "Always loved skating," he added.

"We're looking forward to trying," said Sandy.

"Don't you skate well?" the old man asked Carl and Sandy.

"Only on roller skates," Sandy replied. "But we want to learn as fast as we can."

"I'll teach you," the old man offered. "I began skating about seventy years ago when I was much younger than you two. In fact I skated every opportunity I had. Every afternoon after school and on weekends and vacations from school I skated from dawn to exhaustion."

"Wow!" Carl exclaimed. "You must have been very good!"

The old man smiled as he sat down on the log next to them. "I won the North American championship twice, in 1930 and in 1932. I called my skates the magic blades. They were beautiful skates, different from what you have now. They had long, silvery, tubular blades, black shiny leather, and rawhide laces that stretched and held tight as I turned and spun on the ice."

"Do you still have the skates?" Sandy asked excitedly.

"No," Mr. Bunter answered sadly. "They

disappeared many years ago. I had them in a glass case with my trophies and took them out only to go skating. Someone took them, I guess, and I haven't skated since. I suppose it's foolish to think so, but I could do anything with those skates. They certainly had a special magic for me."

"Do you suppose you could still skate?" Carl asked.

Mr. Bunter bent over and rubbed his eighty-year-old legs. He looked up at the mirrorlike smoothness of the ice, then said solemnly, "No, I guess I'm getting old, but if I had my skates—" He hesitated a moment, then said abruptly, "No, I don't think I could."

Carl and Sandy, with skates laced, carefully walked to the pond edge. Mr. Bunter helped them at first, but soon they were making progress.

Sandy waved good-bye to Mr. Bunter, who hollered, "Don't forget to stop back later for cocoa."

The next few days Carl and Sandy spent every afternoon after school on the pond, skating and listening to Mr. Bunter's advice and tales of his feats on his magic skates. The three became good friends.

One night all the Jensens were browsing around the town's secondhand shop. Suddenly Sandy squealed in delight.

"Oh, Carl!" she called. "Look what I've found!"

On the floor underneath one of the old wooden cases lay a pair of rusty skates. They had long tubular blades, tattered and torn black leather, but no laces. Carl looked at Sandy. They rushed to the counter to buy them.

Mrs. Tremble, the saleswoman, said they could have them for fifty cents. Sandy had a quarter and Carl a dime and two nickels. He rummaged through his pockets but could find only two pieces of bubble gum.

"We only have forty-five cents," Carl said.

Mrs. Tremble smiled warmly and said, "You can have the skates for your forty-five cents."

The children rushed home and immediately began to work on the skates. Sandy was successful in repairing the leather, and a little black shoe polish brought back most of the shine. But no matter how much Carl polished, shined, and buffed, he couldn't make the rust on the blades completely disappear.

Mr. Jensen sharpened the skates on his emery wheel in the cellar, and Mrs. Jensen removed some rawhide from old moccasins for laces. Sandy sat down and typed out a little note.

> *Dear Mr. Bunter,*
> *We have come back! Please try*
> *us out. We've missed you.*
> *The Magic Skates*

They crept up to Mr. Bunter's back door and placed the skates by the door with the note carefully tucked in the laces. Carl motioned for them to leave quietly.

"Do you think those are Mr. Bunter's magic skates, Carl?" Sandy asked.

"Oh, I suppose they're something like his were," Carl said. "There must have been quite a few of those old skates around. Let's get up real early in the morning and see what Mr. Bunter has to say."

The next morning Carl and Sandy ate a hurried breakfast and ran to the pond. When they arrived, they stared in amazement. There on the pond was an old man in a long black coat with a red scarf tied around his chin to keep his battered hat on his head. He seemed to float over the ice in long graceful glides. He wore long tubular black skates with rawhide laces.

"Magic skates," said Sandy.

"For sure," said Carl.

Pocket-size

By S. L. Haenel

"I need water, *malutka*," Yuri's mother said, handing him a pail. His mother often called him this. It meant "little child." Yuri did not mind his mother calling him this, even though he was twelve now, but all the children called him Pocket-size. They said he was so small that he could fit into someone's pocket. Yuri did not think it was very funny.

Yuri ran out of the house to the pump to get the water. They did not have running water in their house like the ones in the city that his brother

Mikhail wrote home about. Mikhail played soccer very well and had become a member of the national team. Yuri hoped that someday he could play as well as his brother. Yuri wanted to be good at *something* so he wouldn't be called Pocket-size, which was why he was so eager to try out this morning for the village soccer club.

He ran back into the house trying not to spill the water. Yuri's mother had fixed his favorite breakfast—potato pancakes. He was too nervous to eat them, though. He set the pail down and looked impatiently at his parents. Finally, his father said, "You may go. We'll see you at the tryouts."

Yuri whooped with joy and ran out of the house and down the dirt road leading to the village. He ran almost all the way to the school field where the tryouts were to be held.

Many of the village boys who had turned twelve recently would be there, including Nikolai and his friends. They were the biggest boys in their grade at school and sometimes pushed the smaller boys and girls around. Nikolai was the first one who had called Yuri Pocket-size.

Coach Anton was a friend of the family. Yuri ran over to him when the boy got to the tryouts. "I wish I were bigger," said Yuri. "I want to do well."

"You shouldn't worry so much," Anton said.

"Being pocket-size is not always so bad. You aren't big or clumsy like some of the others are, you know." Anton moved off to get things ready.

Yuri looked around. The small field was crowded with many young boys Yuri's age and their parents. There were also many officials from the soccer clubs in the area.

"Hey, Pocket-size!" Yuri turned around as he heard his nickname. It was Nikolai. "Do you really think someone so small has a chance, Pocket-size?" Nikolai and a few others laughed at Yuri. He ignored them but wanted to tell them that he could do better than they could anytime. I won't have to listen to the name Pocket-size for long, thought Yuri.

Anton blew a whistle and told everyone who was trying out to line up. The beginners were to line up on the far side of the field with the assistant coach. Everyone who thought he could already play well was to line up near Anton. Yuri ran to the line near the coach and found himself next to Nikolai.

"Aren't you going to line up on the other side, Pocket-size?" Nikolai goaded. His friends laughed, but Yuri just ignored them.

Soon they all started drills. They were tested on how well they could control the ball and how well they could pass it with their feet.

Then Coach Anton announced that they were

going to play a game against some of the team members. The coach and some of the officials divided them into three groups and assigned them positions. Yuri was in the first group and would play forward. He had been given a very important position.

Yuri saw his parents in the crowd, and they waved to him as the players lined up. Nikolai was chosen for the face-off. He did very well, and soon the ball was in his team's control. One of the players passed the ball to Nikolai, who was too far from the goal for a good shot but tried anyway. The goalie stopped the ball easily and threw it to one of his teammates near Yuri.

The boy quickly moved the ball forward. He didn't seem to notice Yuri who ran up beside him and agilely placed his foot in front of the ball, causing it to pop up beside him. Yuri then moved the ball back down the field, trying to dodge the player he had just stolen the ball from. He saw someone near the goal waving his arms. It was Nikolai. Yuri knew that Nikolai was in a good position to score but wished it had been anyone but Nikolai.

Yuri carefully kicked the ball off the side of his foot, across the field to Nikolai, who booted it in for a goal. A whistle blew as Nikolai and some of his friends jumped up and down, patting each other on the back. The coach told them to go to the side, so the next group could take the field.

As Yuri ran off the field, he felt good about the way he had played. It did not matter that Nikolai had scored the goal.

Yuri saw Nikolai running toward him. "Hey, Pocket-size! That was a great play you made."

Yuri was surprised by what Nikolai said. When he called Yuri Pocket-size, it didn't sound mean. Yuri was beginning to think that being small was not really so bad.

"Maybe we could practice on our own sometime. What do you say, Pocket-size?"

"I guess so," was all Yuri could say. He was still surprised but much happier all of a sudden.

At the sideline one man asked Nikolai his name. Then he turned to Yuri. "And what is your name?"

"My name is Yuri," he answered. "But my friends call me Pocket-size!"

Race Against the Clock

By Karen S. Peck

"Good morning, Sarah," Mom called from the hallway. "Get up and look outdoors. Snow day today—no school for you! Why, I bet we've had fifteen inches of snowfall."

Sarah threw back the comforter and scurried to the window. "Oh, no, Mom," she moaned as she looked at the absolute whiteness of her yard.

"What do you mean, 'Oh, no'? No school today— that usually gets a 'Yippee!'" Mom said as she came into Sarah's room.

"I guess I'm not sure how I feel. Today was

supposed to be the three-mile, cross-country ski race at school. The fifth grades had reserved the track for our race. I really wanted to try to break Leslie Olsen's record. She won the sixth-grade competition yesterday by doing the course in thirty minutes. Then again, maybe I'm just as glad we're not racing. I'm not so sure I could do it anyway."

"That doesn't sound like my Sarah to me. I'm sure they'll reschedule your race and you'll get another chance. You just need to think positive. Now do me a favor. Get dressed and go over to Mrs. Davies's and see if she's OK. The phones are out from the storm last night, so I can't make my morning call to her. She's sure to be worried."

"OK," Sarah mumbled, still not certain how to feel about her day off.

Sarah dressed slowly. She ate two muffins and drank a glass of juice before she ventured outside through knee-deep snow to visit their elderly neighbor.

Mrs. Davies was upset when she came to her kitchen door to let Sarah in.

"Oh, look what I've done, dear." She pointed to the floor where a small brown bottle lay broken in a puddle of medicine. "These clumsy old fingers dropped my heart medicine. I tried to call the pharmacy to see if they could deliver another pre-scription, but my phone is dead."

"I know," Sarah said. "That's why I came over.

Mom couldn't get her morning call through. The storm last night knocked down the lines. We're lucky to still have electricity, I guess."

"Oh, what will I do?" Mrs. Davies fussed. "I'm supposed to take that medicine at nine. . . ."

"Gee," Sarah said, "I suppose I could go to the pharmacy for you. But the snow is really deep. It might take me awhile." Then Sarah's eyes brightened. "I could ski there, Mrs. Davies!"

"Oh, would you, dear? Let me write down the prescription number for you." Mrs. Davies carefully picked up the broken bottle and jotted down the number.

On her way out the door Sarah glanced at the clock—it was 8:25. That gave her exactly thirty-five minutes to make the trip and get back by nine. She knew that being a minute or two late probably wouldn't matter much, except that Mrs. Davies was a worrier. Worrying about taking her medicine wouldn't be good for her.

Sarah clumsily waded back to her porch through a deep snowdrift. She traded her heavy parka for a down vest, laced her ski shoes, and told her mom where she was going. Sarah had waxed her skis the night before, after she had practiced. She hoped the wax was extrafast.

While the going was slow at first because of the deep powdery snow, Sarah soon found a snowmobile track to follow. Then she could glide more easily. She soon set a comfortable rhythm for herself, knowing a good pace was important in skiing long distances. Hurrying too fast now would cost her endurance later.

It seemed the entire neighborhood was outdoors. Children were romping in the snow, reveling in their day off from school. Adults were shoveling and blowing driveways clear, which seemed rather foolish to Sarah, since the streets had yet to be plowed.

Sarah arrived at the drugstore, perspiring. She explained Mrs. Davies's problem and handed Mr. Franklin the note.

"I'm really glad you're here, Mr. Franklin," she said. "I just now realized that you might have been stranded at home. Mrs. Davies needs this right away!"

"Oh, I would have been stranded," he answered, "but my neighbor brought me in on a snowmobile. I'll get the prescription in a jiffy."

"Thanks," Sarah said and stood at the counter, shifting her weight from one foot to the other. Don't worry, Mrs. D., she thought, I'm hurrying.

"Here you go," Mr. Franklin said as he handed her the new bottle. "I'll just bill Mrs. Davies for this."

Sarah dashed out of the store, fastened her bindings, and was off. Her wax was holding well, she thought, and the trip back seemed very quick.

She knocked on Mrs. Davies's door. "Here," she said, handing Mrs. Davies the medicine. "Did I make it back in time?"

"Why, yes, dear. It's nine o'clock exactly. Perfect timing! Goodness, you flew those three miles. Come on in and rest a moment, won't you?"

Sarah unfastened her skis and went in. "How far did you say it was to the drugstore?"

"Why, three miles in all—there and back. When Mr. Davies was alive, he used to walk there to get the Sunday paper. I remember him checking the mileage. And you did that distance in only thirty-five minutes!"

Sarah was thinking. Thirty-five minutes—minus about five minutes waiting for the prescription—left thirty minutes. She had skied three miles in thirty minutes! She had tied Leslie's record! In fact, she realized, she had even broken the record! It had been 8:25 when she left to put on her vest and shoes and skis and to tell her mom she was going. That took some time. Then at the pharmacy, she had taken off her skis and put them on again. That took some more time—maybe even four or five minutes in all! She was certain! She had won!

". . . Sarah, are you listening to me?" Mrs. Davies asked. "I offered you a cup of hot chocolate. You seem awfully far away."

"I'm sorry, Mrs. Davies, I guess I was far away. I just won a race! I just broke the school record!"

The Checker Tournament

By Barry Mandell

John sat quietly with his head in his hands. There were just four checkers left on the board, three blacks and one red. The blacks were his, and he had Raymond's only checker in trouble. John's strategy was to close in steadily until he had that last checker. The strategy had worked well during his other games. And skillfully using his last three checkers, he won this game in three moves.

This was John's fourth straight win, and it meant that now he was in the checker-tournament finals of Mr. Berry's third-grade class.

Wow, thought John, twenty-eight kids started out in this tournament on Monday, and now there are just two left, Randy Harris and me.

The boys would play tomorrow, and the winner would get a trophy. John thought a lot about that trophy. But, even more, he thought about how this would show the class he was the best at something.

John knew he wasn't great in reading or writing. And math always gave him trouble. He was pretty good on the playground, but he knew that there were about four others who could run, jump, and play ball better than he could.

But checkers was different. He felt special playing with his twelve pieces. He could even beat his older brother who was in the sixth grade.

After school that day John walked home with his best friend, Peter. "Do you want to get our bikes and ride over to the new science lab they're building?" asked Peter. "We can watch the big cranes."

"Not really," John answered. "I told Mom I'd be home right after school. She's got to do some shopping, and I told her I'd stay home with the baby."

Peter grinned. "I bet you're thinking about that trophy," he said.

"Oh, maybe a little bit," John confessed.

"Well, I'll be rooting for you tomorrow," Peter said as he reached his house and waved goodbye.

"Thanks," John called, managing to smile.

John hardly slept that night. He knew he would have to play the best checkers of his life to beat Randy tomorrow. When he finally fell asleep, he dreamed of great checker moves.

The next day when John came into the classroom, there was a lot of excitement. A checkerboard had been set up on a desk in the middle of the room, and all the chairs had been moved into a circle.

Finally Mr. Berry settled everyone down and announced, "John and Randy have worked hard. They have played excellent checkers to get this far in the tournament. I wish both of them good luck."

Play began. The game moved slowly at first. Neither boy was taking too many chances. A jump here, a jump there. The game continued this way until each boy had four kings left.

John's thoughts occasionally drifted to the trophy. Boy, that sure would look nice in my bedroom. And everyone would think I'm the best.

Suddenly Randy jumped a king and started closing in. The game was now clearly turning in Randy's favor. John tried hard to stay in the game, but he continued to lose one king at a time to Randy's skillful playing. Finally Randy took John's last king, and the game ended.

It was over. John had lost. The class applauded

the two contestants, but John didn't even hear the applause. He went back to his seat and began to cry.

Oh, why was he crying now? He really wasn't a poor sport. But the more he tried to stop, the more he trembled with tears. What would the class think of him now? What would Mr. Berry think?

Suddenly John felt something touch his arm. He lifted his head. Mr. Berry had dropped a note on his desk. Wiping away a tear, he opened the note.

John,

It must be disappointing for you not to win when you've tried so hard and come so close. Crying is often the best way to show your disappointment. But don't feel ashamed. I am proud of you, and the class is proud of you. You may not be the class champ at checkers, but you are a champion person. And I hope you never change.

Mr. Berry

John was still disappointed about not winning, but he was beginning to understand that trying your best was the most important thing. And didn't he always try his best, not only in checkers but in his classes, too?

John walked over to Randy. He put out his hand. "That was a great game," he said. "You deserved to win."

"Thanks," said Randy, shaking John's hand. "You're the best checker player I've ever played against. Think we could do a rematch?"

"Yeah. I'd like that," said John.

When school ended, John left his seat and went to Mr. Berry. He looked at him, and Mr. Berry smiled. John hugged his teacher, a hug that said Thank you.

Peter was waiting outside the room. When John came out, they hurried home to get their bicycles. John just couldn't wait to see those big cranes!

Swimmers, Take Your Mark

By Raymond C. Kartchner

Kelly dived into the water, stretched her arms out in front of her, kicked her feet, and swam for the opposite end of the pool. The water felt good on her body as she cut through it. She increased the speed of her strokes, and very soon her hand touched the other end.

"Hey, let's see you swim across again." The new swim coach was yelling to someone. Kelly looked around to see who he was talking to.

"I mean you." The coach was looking at Kelly.

"You mean me?" Kelly couldn't believe it.

"That's right. You're the one I'm looking at."

"All right." Kelly climbed up on the starting block and prepared for her racing dive. She wanted to go fast, but her knees were shaking so badly that she was afraid they wouldn't even push her into the water. Then all of a sudden she was swimming toward the other side. Her arms and legs felt as if they had big rocks tied to them as she tried to increase her pace.

She finally touched the edge of the pool, shook the water from her eyes, and looked back at the coach. His look was serious. Kelly knew she hadn't swum very fast and wished she hadn't bothered to try. The coach motioned for her to come over, and Kelly walked around the pool biting her lower lip.

"Would you like to be on the team?"

Kelly's eyes blinked. The coach wanted her to be on the team! This was something Kelly hadn't thought possible, and butterflies flew around in her stomach. She wanted to jump in the air and tell everyone.

"Well, would you?" The coach stood waiting.

"You bet I would." Kelly's reply came out fast this time.

"OK, talk to your parents and, if they agree, be at workouts at four on Monday."

"OK, sure, I mean thanks. I'll be here." Kelly ran for the dressing room door and only slowed down a little when she heard the lifeguard yell for her to quit running.

At home, she nearly exploded with the news. "Mom, they want me to swim for the team. The coach asked me. Is it all right? Will it be all right with Dad?"

"We'll have to talk to Dad about it." But Mom's big smile told her that things would work out all right.

On Monday, school went by slowly, and Kelly had a hard time listening to her teachers. She wasn't sure she had any homework. School finally let out, and she raced for home. She bounded into the house and bounced right back out with suit and towel. She was almost to the pool when they got her.

Butterflies.

There were hundreds of little butterflies flying around in her stomach. She always got them when she was "up" for something; but they seemed worse than usual this time, and she was afraid to go in. "It's all right to be afraid as long as you go ahead and try," Kelly whispered. Then she gritted her teeth and went in.

In the swimming pool, the coach introduced her to the other swimmers. They all did lap after lap of freestyle, breast-stroke, and so on. There was advice to keep your elbows out of the water, straighten out your legs, and take more strokes between breaths. Kelly was so tired at the end of the workout that it didn't matter that she had been last to finish in everything.

After Tuesday's workout, the coach called them all together. "There's going to be a swim meet next Saturday, and I've scheduled you in the events where we need you the most." He read the list of swimmers and the events they were to swim. Just as it looked as though the coach had finished, Kelly heard her name called. "Kelly, you will swim the 200-yard freestyle race." Kelly swallowed hard—that was the longest race for her age group, eight lengths of the pool as fast as you could go. She thought maybe the coach had made a mistake, but a look from the coach told her that he had not.

Kelly worked out hard that week. She ate good meals and went to bed early every night. By Friday, she felt better about the meet and her race because she seemed to be doing much better. Her whole family was going to come and watch her swim, and she was determined to make them proud of her. Before she went to sleep Friday night, she imagined what it would be like if she became a swimming champion.

The meet was a big occasion, and there were many swimmers and spectators. Kelly's event was one of the last in the meet, and she was enjoying just being there.

"Swimmers, take your mark." Then, *Pow!* the

starting gun was fired, and six swimmers dived into the water, pulling with all their strength to go as fast as they could. Kelly thought it was too bad that some had to lose because they all tried very hard, and she knew each wanted to win.

Kelly's team was doing pretty well, but her enjoyment began to dwindle when her event was called.

"Swimmers, take your mark." Kelly curled her toes over the edge of the starting block and bent into a crouching position.

Splash! The girl next to Kelly dived in and had to climb back onto the starting block. An official gave the girl a warning, and the process started over again.

"Swimmers, take your mark.". . . *Pow!*

Kelly looked, and every girl was going in. She dived and began to swim with all her might. The yells of the crowd echoed in her ears, and she stroked hard between breaths of air. Before long she was touching the other end. She whirled and looked up—the other swimmers were ahead of her, and she plunged into the next lap determined to go faster than before. After the second lap, she was even farther behind, and her chest was starting to burn for want of more air, but she made her turn and swam. By the end of the fourth lap, Kelly had to breathe on every stroke, and her arms and legs ached.

Come on, Kelly, you can finish, she thought, as she turned and swam.

On this lap her arms got tangled in the lane rope, but she got loose and continued swimming. Six laps gone and she looked up. The fifth-place swimmer was pulling herself out of the water —the rest were already finished. Kelly hesitated just a moment, then started her arms and legs into motion again—two more laps to go. She was the only swimmer now, and she knew she was in last place. With eyes burning and body aching, she swam.

When Kelly finished the race, there were six swimmers on the starting blocks waiting to start the next one. Kelly looked over to where her family was sitting. They were there with big smiles on their faces. Kelly's dad flashed her a **V** sign for victory, and Kelly suddenly felt good all over. She knew there would be other meets and other races. She was determined to train hard. Next time she would do better.

Crotchett's Hill

By William F. Hayes

The day for the race was a scorcher. It was a few minutes before the ten o'clock starting time, and already heat waves radiated from the pavement of the parking lot where the riders were getting ready.

"Think you'll have any problems when you reach Crotchett's Hill?" Jim Hawkins's dad asked.

"Not unless I put too much pressure on all at once," Jim answered. To be safe, he took a wrench from his tool kit and tested the rear-axle nuts. The wheel was firm and hadn't slipped during the week he had practiced zigzagging all the way up Crotchett's Hill instead of attacking it head on.

"Any other problems?" his dad asked.

Jim grinned. "You know the answer to that," he said.

"Thatch Baker?"

"Good guess," Jim said, but his grin got tighter. "Thatch, the winner. Good old Thatch, who would do anything to come in first at anything he tried."

"Can't blame him for that, Jim. Lots of great competitors go out to win."

"Yeah. Well . . ." Jim turned his thoughts to the prize—a chance to spend the day with the Houston Astros. Attend batting practice, the ticket read. Sit in the dugout during a home game. Who wouldn't want that? Jim thought as he wiped the wrench with a rag and stuffed both into the tool kit.

"Still carrying the extra weight of that tool kit around?" Jim turned and saw Thatch Baker astride his stripped-down racing bike.

"Always do," Jim answered.

Thatch laughed. "I can see why," he said. "That old bike doesn't look as if it can stand one more climb up Crotchett's Hill."

"If it breaks down, I can fix it," Jim said.

"Save your energy," Thatch said. "I'm going to win this race."

Jim looked at his father and shrugged just as the starter called the riders to the starting line. From the corner of his eye he saw Thatch join a group of his friends at the far end of the starting line.

The starter raised a gun. "Get set . . ." At the crack of the gun, the riders surged forward.

Jim held back, waiting for the pack to open up in front of him. He pedaled smoothly—humming a tune until his feet picked up the rhythm.

He concentrated on rhythm and pacing, hardly noticing the police cars that cleared the road in front of the cyclists. Jim passed the halfway mark, still concentrating on pacing himself.

"Zowie!" The yell came from behind, and seconds later Thatch pulled alongside him. "Took a wrong turn back there," Thatch shouted and then pulled ahead.

Thatch's confidence made Jim angry. He forgot his pacing and pumped harder until the two of them were abreast.

Thatch laughed. "Save your energy," he shouted and pulled ahead. Soon he was out of sight beyond a bend in the road.

Jim knew Crotchett's Hill was coming up soon, and a fury possessed him. He wanted to win. He wanted to beat Thatch. He wanted to beat everybody. He stood on his pedals—bearing down on them until all the other riders were behind him —except Thatch.

The first sweeping curve of Crotchett's Hill loomed ahead. After the hill there was only half a mile of level road to the finish line. To have a chance, Jim knew he had to reach the top of the hill before Thatch.

The urge to win consumed him. He pedaled furiously but evenly, so he wouldn't strain his bike too much.

Looking up, Jim saw Thatch pulled over on the side of the road. Thatch was tugging at his rear wheel, trying to pull the chain tight. Without a wrench to snug it in position, Thatch was out of the race.

Jim was elated. When he rode past, Thatch just shrugged his shoulders.

At that moment the elation died. Jim wanted to win, but not like this. He turned back.

Jim didn't speak. He took some tools from his kit and handed them to Thatch. He paid no attention when Thatch pointed out other racers walking their bikes up the hill.

"Your old clunker will never catch up," Thatch said, setting to work on the chain.

"All I can do is try," said Jim, pedaling away as hard as he could.

"You don't stand a chance of catching them now," Thatch said a minute later as he sailed past. "But I do." And with a roaring cry he pedaled furiously up to the top of the hill.

Jim, still determined to make a race of it, pumped harder. The kerchunk of his chain snapping off the sprocket told him all was lost. When he looked up, he saw the last of the bike-walkers top the hill with Thatch close behind.

The prize ticket had already been awarded by the time Jim crossed the finish line. Thatch and his group of friends were jumping around and hollering so much that Jim figured one of them had won. It was Thatch.

"Half of this prize really belongs to you," said Thatch.

"No, you earned it," Jim said with a smile.

That evening at home Jim was still thinking about the race. It hurt to lose—there was no denying that. But Jim had come to a conclusion. He could get over losing a whole lot quicker than he could have gotten over winning if he hadn't stopped to help Thatch. Besides, there was always next year's race.

First Mackerel

By Orlo Strunk

Debbie wondered if anyone in the family knew just how much she wanted to catch the first mackerel of the year.

"It's a perfect day for mackerel fishing," Mr. Hull, Debbie's father, said as he sipped his breakfast coffee. "The mackerel are moving. They're out there. Yesterday while hauling my lobster traps I saw several schools—fine, big ones, too."

"And I'm ready for them!" Sid, Debbie's older brother, said proudly, probably remembering last year when he had caught the first mackerel of the year, a big one nearly twenty inches long.

Mother left the stove and joined the family at the table.

"Personally," she said, smiling, "I think it's time for the women in this family to win the mackerel fishing game."

The twins, Barb and Bea, liked that. They laughed as they spread jam on the toast for the whole family.

Debbie laughed with them. This would be the fifth year she could remember trying to catch the flashing fish. She had joined the family game on her fifth birthday. Last year a mackerel had hit her silver jig just as her big brother had landed a large mackerel on the deck of the *Splinter,* her father's lobster boat. Debbie had missed catching the mackerel by just a few seconds. She remembered now how she had felt—both sad and happy at the same time. She could not help but laugh at her older brother's victory dance all around the deck. At the same time, she had come so very close to landing the first mackerel herself that she felt disappointed and sad.

"You came close last year," Father said, as if he could read Debbie's mind.

"Three seconds late," Debbie managed to say, holding three fingers up for everyone to see.

Sid laughed. "Debbie should win this year the way she's been shining her jig the past week. It has more sparkle than Ma's best silver."

The whole family laughed, and Father, ruffling Debbie's blonde hair, said, "Good idea, Debbie. And just remember: Keep your line wet and your jig jumping."

Debbie was thinking of her father's advice later in the morning as the *Splinter* cut its way through the morning swells. It was indeed an ideal day. The sun was bright, the sky totally blue, and the ocean a calm green. The lobster boat, scrubbed clean for the occasion, seemed almost like a pleasure yacht as its bow sliced its way toward the one-mile buoy.

Debbie reviewed the game in her mind. Her father would turn off the engine when he thought they were anywhere near a school of mackerel. The *Splinter* would drift quietly on the green swells, hopefully right over a school of hungry mackerel.

It was always Father who gave the signal for the game to start. Soon after the engine stopped, he would come to the stern of the boat where everyone was ready with poles and jigs. He'd shout, "First mackerel of the year!" Then six jigs would splash into the ocean and as many poles would begin to jump up and down. And then . . .

But Debbie's thoughts were interrupted by the sudden silence. The engine had stopped!

"Should be around here someplace," Father said, taking his own short rod in his hands.

Sid was already poised, his fishing rod in one hand, a silver jig in the other. The twins and Mother were also ready. As Debbie held her brightly polished jig between her fingers, she could feel the excitement mount. She could even hear her heart pounding in her ears.

"First mackerel of the year!"

Before Father's voice faded, the family's jigs were in the water, sinking toward the bottom.

Debbie decided to let her jig sink all the way to the bottom, bump it up and down five or six times, then reel it up a few feet and jerk it up and down some more.

"There's no telling how deep they are," Sid reminded everyone as he lifted and lowered his pole quickly.

Debbie tried to watch the others out of the corners of her eyes, at the same time keeping her jig moving up and down. Apparently, the *Splinter* hadn't found the mackerel yet, or the jigs were down too far, or not far enough.

Debbie and the others fell silent, concentrating intently on their jigging.

Suddenly, about a hundred yards off the starboard bow of the boat, the ocean seemed to explode.

"Tuna! Tuna!" Father shouted, pointing.

Debbie stole a quick glance, just enough to see the sharp fins of a dozen tuna break the surface of the ocean, splashing water in all directions.

The twins screamed gleefully at the sight, quickly reeling up their lines as if afraid one of the big tuna would take their jigs. Sid seemed spellbound by the leaping tuna, his pole lowered and still. Even Father and Mother had stopped jigging their jigs.

But Debbie continued to lift and lower her rod, jigging furiously.

And then she felt the steady jerking at the other end of the line, and she knew she had a mackerel.

Quickly she began to reel in, feeling the frantic run of the mackerel move up and down her arms like an electric current. Could she land it now that it was hooked? She played it carefully, trying not to jerk the single hook from the mouth of the darting, diving fish.

Then she saw it—and with one smooth lift of the rod she tossed the flapping mackerel onto the deck.

"Debbie gets the first mackerel of the year!" Father announced, holding the prize fish up for all to see.

That evening at their traditional mackerel dinner, Debbie felt good all over. Sid put a brotherly hand on her shoulder. "I think," he said, "we should have a speech from this year's winner. I give you the mackerel-fishing champion of the family, Debbie Hull!"

Debbie felt her face flush. She had never given a speech before. But then, remembering how the rest of the family had been distracted by the splashing tuna, she stood up, cleared her throat, and said:

"Nothing to it, folks—just keep your line wet and your jig jumping—and the tuna coming!"

Super Shrimp

By Stephanie Moody

Smack-smack, smack-smack. The basketball players dribbled the big orange ball down the court, looking for a chance to score a basket.

Danny held his breath, squeezing his hands together as he watched the ball arch upward, then down, swishing through the net. Jumping to his feet, Danny cheered and clapped with the rest of the crowd. His team had scored. They were ahead at last.

Soon Danny would be able to play. A few more

points. A few more minutes. Then it would be his turn to play.

Danny knew he wasn't the best player on the team. But oh how he wanted to be. Thinking about it made his skin tingle—the hush of the crowd as he paused to shoot, the building excitement as the ball looped into the net for the winning score, the wild cheering. If only . . . if only . . .

Danny shook his head, clearing away his daydream. He needed to be alert when the coach called on him, not off somewhere else dreaming the impossible.

"Okay, Shrimp, you're in for Juggler Johnson." Danny's nickname stung, even if it was true. Compared to the others, he was a shrimp. Everybody on the team called him Shrimp or Pip-Squeak. Of course, they had nicknames, too, like Juggler, Flash, or Sure-Shot. But theirs weren't names to grow out of. They had names that fit them like well-worn shoes.

Tagging Juggler, Danny took his spot in the lineup. Today would be different, he told himself. Today he'd be *so* good, no, he'd be so *great*, that his size wouldn't matter.

A hand-off from Sure-Shot Nichols got Danny into the action fast. He pivoted left and then charged right, throwing his guard off-balance and setting up a pass back to Sure-Shot. Danny grinned. He wasn't tall, but he was quick, he told himself, like a distant flash of lightning: gone before you knew it was there.

Settling into the pace of the game, Danny looked for openings where he could show his stuff, but the game seemed to take place above him and beyond his reach. Rebounds were grabbed by taller players. Long passes were intercepted. His shots fell short of their mark.

Eying the scoreboard, Danny brushed the sweat from his forehead. The clock read 2:58, and the score was tied. How had *that* happened? The coach only let him play when they were safely ahead. Why didn't he send in a taller player?

A foul stopped play, giving Danny a needed moment to think. There must be a reason, he told himself, a reason the coach had left him in. "Look for their weaknesses," his coach had said before the game. "Know what you do best, and do it."

"Best? Best?" Danny mumbled out loud as the ball found the hoop on the single free throw, pushing the other team ahead by one point. "I'm the best at being small, but that's . . ." Danny didn't need to finish. He had the answer.

As the others reached for a missed jump shot, Danny held back, waiting for his moment. When it came, he exploded into action.

Making himself as small as possible, Danny snatched the dribbled ball from under his opponent. It was a snap. The other player hadn't seen Danny coming. He was too tall.

Now Danny was playing at *his* level, one the other team wasn't used to. Danny limited himself to quick moves, short passes. He didn't pass high. He passed low, setting up his teammates for baskets. The score swung back and forth.

As the final seconds ticked off the clock, Danny spun left toward the basket, keeping the ball close to his chest. Now was the time for him to score the winning basket, to hear the crowd cheer, to feel the glory. A guard loomed above him, daring Danny to shoot. Just as the guard jumped, Danny saw his opening. But instead of shooting, he bounce-passed the ball to Sure-Shot right between the guard's legs. Sure-Shot proved true to his name. He put the ball up and in as the buzzer sounded. His basket had won the game.

Happy fans hoisted Sure-Shot up on their shoulders, yelling their praise, but not before he grabbed Danny in a bear hug. "Great playing, Shrimp. You were super!"

Danny's face flushed with pleasure. He was a shrimp, all right. A Super Shrimp.

A Team Needs a Hero

By Neil C. Fitzgerald

Adam Morris crouched, hands on knees, peering in at the Wildcats' batter. Adam knew the score. With only one out, another big hit would mean the Cardinals could wave good-bye to the league championship. Trailing by one run going into the last half inning wouldn't be too bad. But another two or three runs might be just too much to overcome.

The Cardinals' pitcher received the sign from his catcher. The Wildcats' runners led off from each base. Adam measured the distance between himself and the third-base bag. The pitcher took a full windup and fired. The batter swung and stung the ball. Adam dived to his right, flashed out his glove, and backhanded the hard grounder. He stepped on third and whipped the ball across the diamond to first. Double play!

Adam trotted to the bench with the sweet sound of cheers ringing in his ears. His teammates kept slapping him on the back. "Great play, Adam," said Coach Bolton. The three words really pleased Adam. Coach Bolton was his hero.

Adam remembered listening to the final game of the college world series when "Red" Bolton, as he was called then, won the championship game for his team with a game-winning hit. Everyone thought Red would give the pros a try. Instead he returned to his hometown, took a teaching position, and began a coaching career.

Adam's play had given the Cardinals a lift. Spirits on the bench were high. "All right, you guys," shouted Coach Bolton, "one run to tie and two to win. Let's do it!"

All the boys took up the cry. "Let's do it!"

When the lead-off hitter for the Cardinals tapped a slow grounder back to the pitcher, the cry for victory softened. But then a walk and a scratch single brought everyone off the bench. The Cardinal fans rose to their feet.

Adam reached over and picked up his favorite bat. He walked out to the on-deck circle and knelt down. His pal Peter was the next hitter. Adam hoped Peter could drive in the tying run and leave the winning run for him. Wouldn't that be some finish!

Peter took a ball low. The relief pitcher for the Wildcats was humming the ball. Peter choked up on the bat and slashed at the next pitch. He caught the ball on the end of the bat and sent a grounder bounding between first and second. The Wildcat second baseman darted to his left, scooped up the ball, and flipped it to first. Two out, runners on second and third.

Adam sauntered up to the plate. He took a deep breath and stepped into the batter's box. "Come on, Adam! You can do it, boy!" Adam heard the voices raining down upon him.

Adam stared at the Wildcats' pitcher. Adam knew this pitcher had the best fastball in the league. But Adam had been feasting on fastballs all season. He also knew the pitcher could afford to walk him with first base open. Adam was determined to get his pitch.

The pitcher took a full windup and let loose. The ball sailed high, forcing the catcher to reach up for the ball. Adam never moved. Once again the pitcher fired. Adam leaned back. "Strike!" shouted the umpire.

Adam stepped away from the plate. The umpire thought the ball had caught the inside corner of the plate. Adam shook his head and reached down for a handful of dirt. His hands were starting to sweat.

Adam stepped back in and fixed his gaze on the pitcher. Adam knew his pitcher. Guard the outside corner, Adam said to himself. The pitcher leaned back. The arm came forward. Adam swung. Bat met ball. A liner shot toward the first baseman. He dived toward the line. The ball whistled past him. "Foul ball!" screamed the umpire as Adam broke toward first.

Adam returned to the batter's box. He could hit this guy's fastball. He would drive the next one into fair territory. The crowd hushed. The pitcher walked around the mound. Adam waited, poised and alert. The pitcher got the sign and took his stance. Once more he began the big windup and brought the arm forward.

Adam was ready. Too ready. The ball didn't hum—it floated like a small white balloon. Adam was committed. He lunged at the ball, trying at the same time to pull back. The ball drifted over the plate. The umpire shot his right arm up into the air. "Strike!"

The groans were like thunder. Adam felt every one of them. He was stunned. His dreams lay shattered around him. Head lowered, he plodded back to the bench and sat down in utter dejection. His eyes never left the ground.

Adam wasn't aware that someone was beside him until Coach Bolton spoke. "It happened to me, you know. Twice." Adam looked up at his coach through gathering tears. "Yes," continued Coach Bolton, "and I can still feel the pain. Once in high school and once in the college world series."

Adam frowned. "But you were the star of the college world series. Everyone knows you won the championship game with a hit in the last of the ninth."

Coach Bolton smiled. "Yes, in my senior year. That was sweet. But as a junior in a quarterfinal game I was up just like you, with runners on second and third, two outs, and trailing by one run."

"What happened, Coach?"

"There were two strikes on me. I swung at the next pitch and hit nothing but air. So don't get down on yourself, you hear?"

Adam wiped his eyes with the sleeve of his uniform. "Yeah, Coach, I hear." Adam stood up and headed for the team bus. Coach Bolton put his arm around Adam and walked along beside him. No doubt about it, Adam thought, Coach Bolton is some kind of hero.

Happy Skates

By Diane Burns

The skating rink is a big cookie-shape with people clumped like frosting around it. I'm ready to skate my Dance of the Toys. My feet can't help jiggling. My stomach jiggles, too.

"Our second skater is Mavie Brown." The announcer's voice booms loud enough to crack the ice.

My coach, Miss Jordan, hugs me and says, "Go, Happy Skates. No Show-Off Skates today."

Show-Off Skates can make me fall. Happy Skates don't. But sometimes I can't tell the difference until I stumble.

I step onto the ice, and the cold air kisses my face. The same bright light that followed the first skater is following me. It's warm, like Miss Jordan's voice. Everyone is watching me. It's *my* turn!

The music starts. *Ta-Tum! Ta-Tum!* I am a toy soldier skating to stiff drum music. I skate forward, then backward. I swivel on one skate. Back and forth I march. Happy Skates are careful skates, so I only wobble a little. The crowd cheers. My Happy Skates go faster.

Skate, glide. Toy-soldier music changes to jewelry-box music. I circle my arms over my head and skate on one foot. I stretch the other foot behind me. I am a dancing-doll ballerina. The crowd cheers louder, and my skates speed along.

Now I am a toy bunny, hopping to bouncy music. The bright light hops with me. The crowd claps, and I turn too fast toward the center of the ice. Those Show-Off Skates make me sit down hard! When I try to get up, I fall down again. And again. Maybe it doesn't hurt a toy bunny's knee to go bump on the ice, but it hurts mine. The crowd holds its breath and waits. My music zooms on, flying like a toy airplane. But my dance isn't flying anymore.

Slowly, I stand up. The crowd whistles and claps. Very carefully, I start to skate. I circle once around the whole cookie-rink, rubbing my knee. My skate blades sing: "Happy . . . skates . . . happy . . . skates." They will not show off anymore. I am glad of that, but now it is too late. My music is finished. Because of Show-Off Skates, I have missed my toy airplane dance.

Everyone thinks I am done because my music is done. They will be sad that I skated only three toy dances when I wanted to do four. But my skates have a surprise for everyone. The bright light follows me out to the middle of the ice.

I glide carefully on my Happy Skates. When I am going fast, but not *too* fast, I start to twirl. The crowd blurs together like a merry-go-round. Around and around I spin. My skate blades crunch into the ice. The wind whistles music in my ears. My arms catch the warm, bright light. Happy Skates twirl! I twirl! I am a twirling toy top.

Too soon, the wonderful spin is over. My knee still hurts, but I bow anyway before I leave the ice. The crowd's cheering wraps me in a giant hug. I have Happy Skates on my feet and a happy smile on my face.

The next skater glides onto the ice. Her skates are jiggling, just the way mine did. I know all about jiggling feet.

"Go, Happy Skates!" I yell.